For Doug
—B. B.

To Sarah
—D. S.

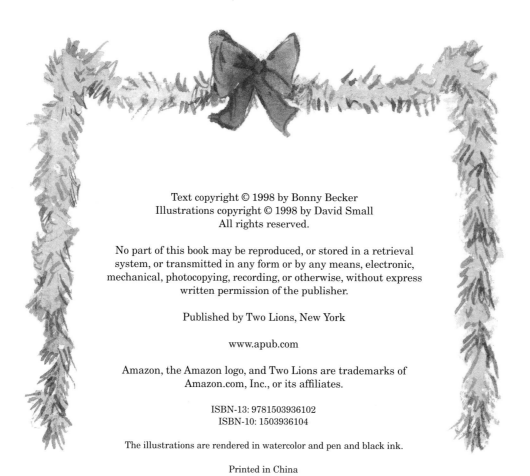

Published by Two Lions, New York

www.apub.com

Amazon, the Amazon logo, and Two Lions are trademarks of
Amazon.com, Inc., or its affiliates.

ISBN-13: 9781503936102
ISBN-10: 1503936104

The illustrations are rendered in watercolor and pen and black ink.

Printed in China

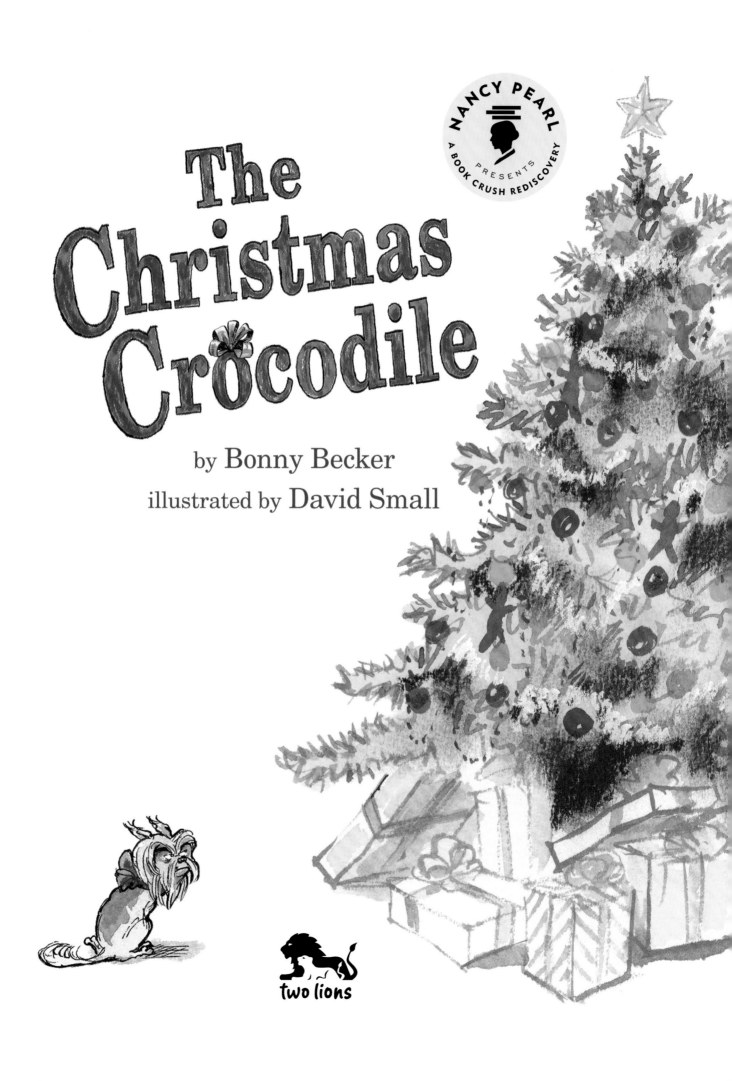

The Christmas Crocodile

by Bonny Becker

illustrated by David Small

two lions

Introduction
by Nancy Pearl

A great picture book comes into being when a wonderfully told story meets illustrations that both complement the author's words and add depth and texture to the tale. Of course there are also many marvelous books where writer and illustrator are one and the same. Three of my favorite authors who both write and illustrate their books are Maurice Sendak (especially *Where the Wild Things Are*), Chris Van Allsburg (especially *The Garden of Abdul Gasazi*), and Robert McCloskey (especially *Make Way for Ducklings*).

Bonny Becker, the author of *The Christmas Crocodile*, and I sat down together on one unexpectedly and unusual beautiful Seattle morning in November to talk about her experience writing and publishing this book. What's always been interesting to me is that, most of the time, the authors don't choose (or often have any input into) who is going to illustrate the book. That was the case with *The Christmas Crocodile*. It was sent to David Small by her publisher. And, as you'll see the moment you open *The Christmas Crocodile*, the combination of writer Bonny Becker and illustrator David Small was clearly a match made in heaven.

When *The Christmas Crocodile* was published in 1998, Judith Viorst (who wrote, among other books for children, *Alexander and the Terrible, Horrible, No Good, Very Bad Day*) gave it a rave review in the Dec. 6, 1998 issue of *The New York Times Book Review*, calling it "outrageous and hilarious." Daniel Pinkwater (author of *The Snarkout Boys & the Avocado of Death* as well as many other books for kids and teens) read it on his *Chinwag Theater* show on National Public Radio.

Becker told me that the idea for *The Christmas Crocodile* started off—in 1989— as a rhymed verse about a crocodile who wanted to eat the Christmas tree and his friend, Missy Franklin. Becker worked on the poem for years, and it slowly morphed into the book we have today, which features a little girl named Alice Jayne who finds a voraciously hungry crocodile (with a bright-red bow around his neck) under the Christmas tree. (Becker remembered later that's exactly how she found the dachshund puppy she had gotten in fourth grade.) As Alice Jayne soon discovers, her new friend can't stop himself from eating everything he encounters, including, but not limited to, shoes, a roast, a box of candy, the bright-red ribbon that was once tied around his neck, a hot water bottle, and the left stove-top burner. Interestingly, "The Christmas Crocodile didn't mean to be bad, not really," which is the sentence that opens the book and is repeated throughout, was the last line that came to Becker as she worked on the book.

There's nothing in the text of *The Christmas Crocodile* to indicate when the events take place. It was illustrator David Small's brilliant decision to set the book during the Edwardian period, roughly the first decade of the twentieth century. His humorous drawings of Alice Jayne, her parents, her cousin Elwood, and her Aunt Figgy and Uncle Theodore—not to mention the crocodile—take Becker's words and make them sing.

The Christmas Crocodile is perfect for children ages 4 to 8. Becker told me that one of her favorite questions to ask children who have read *The Christmas Crocodile* is what they think the egg on the last (wordless) page of the book will hatch into. (There's a hint on the back endpapers.)

I'm thrilled that *The Christmas Crocodile* is part of the Book Crush Rediscoveries series. I hope you and your children love it as much as I do.

Here are some other picture books whose illustrations perfectly complement their texts:
Verna Aardema's *Why Mosquitoes Buzz in People's Ears: A West African Tale*,
    illustrated by Leo and Diane Dillon
Bonny Becker's *A Visitor for Bear*, illustrated by Kady MacDonald Denton
Karen Henry Clark's *Sweet Moon Baby*, illustrated by Patrice Barton
Ezra Jack Keats's *The Snowy Day*, illustrated by the author
Barbara McClintock's *Adèle & Simon*, illustrated by the author
Ted Kooser's *House Held Up By Trees*, illustrated by Jon Klassen
David Small's *Imogene's Antlers*, illustrated by the author

The Christmas Crocodile didn't mean to be bad, not really. Alice Jayne found him on Christmas Eve under the tree. He wore a red bow around his neck. It was lovely. Except he ate it.

Then he ate a couple of presents, just little ones,
and he gnawed on Father's shoe, ate the wreath in the hall,
and ran away with the Christmas roast—a big one. He was
eating up Christmas and no one knew what to do with him.

"Send the beast to Africa," huffed Uncle Theodore, who had once hunted wild game there.

"He must be put in an orphanage," fretted Aunt Figgy, who worried a lot, especially about orphans.

"Lock him in the back room, Alice Jayne," instructed Father, "while we consider the situation."

"Better give him the pumpkin pie," said Mother. "He still looks hungry."

Alice Jayne crossed her arms and tapped her toe while the Christmas Crocodile slunk into the back room. She closed and locked the door with a firm click.

But then she thought she heard him sniffling in there. Not feeling
hungry after all, she slipped him the pineapple upside-down cake,
along with the pie.

"We could make him into a pair of shoes," said Uncle Theodore, who was busy considering things back in the parlor.

"Or a pet for some orphans," said Aunt Figgy.

"I wonder whose presents he ate?" said Cousin Elwood, who had finally finished eating all the fudge the Crocodile had missed and could now speak.

"He's nice," said Alice Jayne. "Maybe we could keep him."

"Unheard of!" protested Aunt Figgy.

"But it's Christmas," said Alice Jayne.

"Irrelevant," harrumphed Uncle Theodore.

"He's just a little hungry, that's all," said Alice Jayne.

"Perhaps the zoo would take him," said Father, worriedly.

"He needs a real home!" cried Alice Jayne.

"We'll think about it, dear," said Mother, and she sent them all to bed.

The Christmas Crocodile didn't mean to be bad, not really. But in the middle of the night he ate through the back room door, swallowed twenty-nine crumpets on the kitchen counter, a box of pralines, one fruitcake, five golden oranges, the left stove-top burner, and a plate of ginger star cookies—they were for Santa!

Then he crept upstairs. One door was open just a bit. He nuzzled it open a bit more. Inside, he found tasty talcum powder, a feather boa that tickled his tongue, and a swig of perfume. *Just right!* Then he found ten pink toes. He sniffed them. *Hmmmmm.* He licked them. *Yummmmm.* He took a teeny, tiny bite.

Aunt Figgy's scream shivered cobwebs in the attic,
and made the dust dance on a bottle of wine in the cellar.

"I'll save you!" roared Uncle Theodore, waking with a start from
a dream about cannibals.

"Run for your lives!" shrieked Cousin Elwood.

"There's blood!" gasped Aunt Figgy, pointing to a pinprick of red
on her little toe.

"Where is he?" sighed Mother.

The Christmas Crocodile didn't mean to be bad, not really.
They found him hiding under Alice Jayne's bed. He tried to wag
his tail in a friendly fashion, but it was too cramped.

"Into the cellar with him!" commanded Father.

The Christmas Crocodile scooted sadly down the stairs to the basement. He shivered in the cold, but Alice Jayne crossed her arms and tapped her toe. She closed and locked the door with a firm click.

She went back to bed and lay under her warm blanket. She swallowed a lump in her throat.

Somehow it didn't feel like the night before Christmas anymore.

She slipped out of bed, her blanket held close, and crept quietly
down the stairs to the basement.

She wrapped the Crocodile snugly, tucking her blanket under
his chin. She found an old candy cane, covered with lint, in her
bathrobe pocket. She broke it in two.

"One for me and one for you," she whispered.

The Christmas Crocodile gulped happily and closed his eyes.

The cellar door creaked open.

"You know, he could be an orphan," hissed Aunt Figgy, slipping inside. She tucked her hot water bottle under the Crocodile's toes.

"A crocodile saved my life once," announced Uncle Theodore, coming in behind Aunt Figgy. "Decent chap, really." He spread his Zulu robe over the Crocodile's tail.

"Perhaps he's learned his lesson," said Father, peering around the door and holding up his red earmuffs.

"Is it time to open presents yet?" yawned Cousin Elwood, stumbling in. He patted the Crocodile on the snout and fell asleep.

Mother came last. She spread a fluffy comforter across them all.
"We couldn't leave him alone," she said. "Not on Christmas Eve."
Everyone nodded.
The Christmas Crocodile let out a contented snore.
"Full at last," observed Father.
Everyone sighed.
Then they all settled down to wait . . .
. . . and watch.

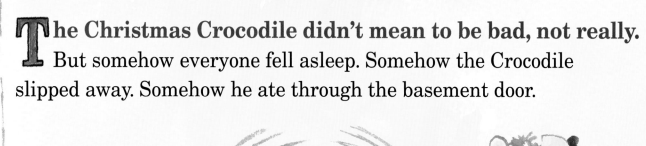

The Christmas Crocodile didn't mean to be bad, not really.
But somehow everyone fell asleep. Somehow the Crocodile
slipped away. Somehow he ate through the basement door.

They found him the next morning in the parlor,
looking alarmingly round.

Alice Jayne's blanket was gone.
Aunt Figgy's hot water bottle was gone.
Uncle Theodore's Zulu robe was gone.
Father's earmuffs were gone.
Mother's comforter was gone.
The Christmas tree was gone (a blue spruce!).
All the presents were gone . . . except one.

"Pump his stomach!" yowled Elwood.
"Send for my elephant gun!" roared Uncle Theodore.
"Those were for the orphans!" shrieked Aunt Figgy
about the missing presents.

"What's that?" asked Alice Jayne, pointing at the one small present remaining.

"If he didn't want it, it must be bad," Cousin Elwood announced.

"Quite so," agreed Uncle Theodore. Aunt Figgy nodded.

"I'll open it," said Alice Jayne, and she quickly tore off the ribbon.

"It's from Uncle Carbuncle!"
cried Cousin Elwood.

"Good old Carbuncle,"
shouted Uncle Theodore.

"Carbuncle, at last," breathed Aunt Figgy.

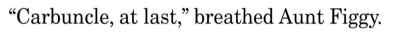

"But we haven't got an Uncle Carbuncle,"
protested Alice Jayne.

Since she was right, no one knew what to
say. But Alice Jayne knew. It meant that the
Christmas Crocodile had been delivered to
the wrong address.

And sure enough, the doorbell rang.

At the door were two deliverymen.

"Take him away," Father said, firmly.

The two men hoisted up the Crocodile and
staggered down the snowy steps to a waiting van.

"Good-bye," said Alice Jayne, sadly.

The Christmas Crocodile snuffled. One great crocodile tear ran
down his snout. But then he saw the sign on the delivery van.

"I'll come visit soon," promised Alice Jayne as they loaded him into the van.

"Merry Christmas!" cried the deliverymen.

"Merry Christmas!" cried one and all.

The Christmas Crocodile didn't mean to be bad, not really. He waved his tail farewell, but, as the van rounded the corner, it did look rather like a deliveryman's cap in his jaws.

"Well," sighed Mother, "peace at last."
"Yes," agreed everyone . . .
. . . except Alice Jayne, who didn't say a word.